This Is A Dreamland

Tathagata Banerjee

Ukiyoto Publishing

All global publishing rights are held by

Ukiyoto Publishing

Published in 2024

Content Copyright ©Tathagata Banerjee

ISBN 9789364945806

All rights reserved.

No part of this publication may be reproduced, transmitted, or stored in a retrieval system, in any form by any means, electronic, mechanical, photocopying, recording or otherwise, without the prior permission of the publisher.

The moral rights of the author have been asserted.

This is a work of fiction. Names, characters, businesses, places, events, locales, and incidents are either the products of the author's imagination or used in a fictitious manner. Any resemblance to actual persons, living or dead, or actual events is purely coincidental.

This book is sold subject to the condition that it shall not by way of trade or otherwise, be lent, resold, hired out or otherwise circulated, without the publisher's prior consent, in any form of binding or cover other than that in which it is published.

www.ukiyoto.com

To all who fight the good fight and get into the good trouble to defend the truth

"For when my outward action doth demonstrate
The native act and figure of my heart
In complement extern, 'tis not long after
But I will wear my heart upon my sleeve
For daws to peck at. I am not what I am."

- *Iago, 'Othello, the Moor of Venice',*
- *William Shakespeare.*

Contents

Neon Xity	1
Redgarden Xity	3
Worldstage	6
Revolution	9
Home	11
Stranger	13
The Lawyer	16
Xity-Five Osmosis	20
Kapitol	23
The Committee	26
Alliance	30
War	34
IAGO	38
People	43
About the Author	*45*

Neon Xity

"**O**rwell is dead. We've killed him."

The chant was echoing through the streets of WorldStage, subsection 136. A calm statement being uttered by innumerable people on the roads. Not a threatening tone. Just a fact being put forward. Indeed, Orwell was dead.

The book burning ceremony is the biggest festivity of the people of WorldStage. There's this humongous statue in the Kapitol - the nation's capital city - where this crowd will march to. The statue is of Iago - a character created by Shakespeare back in his day. Shakespeare drew him as a villain. In the modern world, Iago had been interpreted as the hero - the poster boy of how propaganda succeeds. The statue is accompanied by a decorated plaque with the words engraved - "I AM NOT WHAT I AM." It's something he said in the original play. The crowd will gather here and burn the books. Education is outlawed now for the common people. Non-conformity is outlawed now. And because Orwell thought this would happen, even he's outlawed now.

This is WorldStage. The dawn of a new civilization. Everything is good here. No one thinks, so no one suffers. Happy times are all that people have. Time has frozen up here. Everything is peaceful. Everyone is oblivious.

Sam could hear the sounds from his workspace. His holiday for the Book Burning Season is beginning from tomorrow. He was looking forward to it. The workload had been hectic. He leaned back in his chair. What year is it now? There's no record left since 2075. And even that has been like a hundred or so years ago. WorldStage was their little country. A happy place. Sure, there were diseases which killed crores of people every year. And yes, sure, there were famines every few months which would cost lives of uncountable citizens. But they were - Sam sighed with a relief - poor people who died. And who cares when poor people die. The rich need to get richer. That is how you change the world. One day, only rich people will remain. And then, there's your Utopia. Eternal peace. WorldStage gives the chance to evolve. Work hard. Work hard at the mining plants, at the sweatshops, at the farm. Work hard to make the rich even richer. And one day, you might get rich too. It's all pure calculated math. Economy at its finest form.

The point was, WorldStage was a great country to be in. What was happening outside of it? They don't know. Who needs to know, really? What's the point of knowledge, especially when there's no place to utilise it. Sam felt content as he looked on at the street. Descartes said one exists because one thinks. Like most people, he was wrong. This is right, Sam thought. Burning books is right. Not thinking is right. What is happening in WorldStage? What happens to other people? Where is humanity? How's the financial condition of this place? Would anyone even survive to see the next year? Does the grander world outside of WorldStage work in any different way than them? These are the questions he didn't care for. No one did. As far as they were concerned, there's nothing outside of this place. The world begins and ends with this place - hey, the word 'world' is literally there in WorldStage. And it's all good.

WorldStage is where he has always been, and it'll always be the place where he'd be. He'd never be anywhere else. His entire life is perfectly captured like a frame in this place. Sam felt a little bit uncomfortable with his train of thought. He's... He's gonna be here forever, and will not know anything beyond it. WorldStage sounds a lot like a horrific prison when one puts it that way. Sam brushes the thought off. No, that can't be it. This is home. They're all happy here.

Sam looked at the outside again. Subsection 136 was the formal name of this place, the unofficial name being Neon Xity. The marching crowd will travel cross country to go to the Kapitol, where people from other cities will also come. It's a festival that goes on for days. There has been drizzle since the morning. Sam took out the raincoat from his bag. The Neon Xity Subway is a bit far from his workplace. He needed to walk, and he didn't want to get wet.

Sam smiled to himself. It's a good day.

Redgarden Xity

The rainfall has a pattern. Coherence. Symmetry. She liked that about everything. Things need to be systematic in order to function properly.

Stana could hear the sounds as the car was going through the roads of RedGarden Xity. It was night, and the darkened glasses of the car were blocking the view outside. She smiled. Well, if one had to go out, this is a fantastic way. A rebel.

The Book Burning Ceremony attracts protesters every year. Despite the law and bans, a lot of people end up having a mind of their own after all. Police had been reformed as a branch of militarized army, and they took the protesters under arrest. They would be produced in front of the court, which would inevitably find the individuals as terrorists. The convicts are sentenced to varying kinds of punishment - either a life imprisonment or a death penalty. Stana laughed to herself. It's all a facade, a pretension of a system taking its course. The arrests, the law - it's all a ploy to continue to present WorldStage as a democracy. It's a full-blown dictatorship. Everyone knows that. A few people stand up, and perish.

The raindrops were hitting the pavements as the car zoomed past. Stana pushed her hair back. Some people stand up. Some people like her. She had been arrested at the book burning ceremony earlier today, protesting against the system and the people in power. This guarded police van would be taking her to the police station. And then... She sighed... And then, there's no turning back. There would be incessant media reporting. The media in WorldStage is a powerful tool. It doesn't lie. It doesn't distort the truth. It amplifies the truth to the level of fiction. It's an artform, she often thought in grudging amusement. Facts of one's life would be presented so brilliantly that simple truth will give birth to a grand false narrative. The media sustains the autocracy here. It's a masterful move, Stana thought. There's no top figure in the controlling body of WorldStage. If there is no dictator, none can call it a dictatorship in the first place. The country is controlled by The Committee, an organization which rules everything. The top figures of The Committee take important decisions. The battens change hands. A facade, she thought again, of a system.

There are CCTV cameras in every corner of RedGarden Xity. The armed guards patrol the areas. A flying helicopter of the police roams over the city every so often. Stana tried to understand exactly where she was. The police van is consisting of three people plus the driver. Two armed officers in bikes were by the side. She saw it when she was thrown into the car. Stana sat up straight. Depending on the speed, she had tried to calculate how far they'd come. She knew the road towards the station. Stana calmed her nerves. If she's right, they're at the blindspot. And things should start to begin now.

A few seconds passed. A slow sound, and the area suddenly got filled up with smoak. The car suddenly came to a crashing halt, hitting the empty shop nearby, shattering the glass window. A tremendously loud cranking noise on the door, and the van opened up.

"Come out, we've three seconds!"

Stana jumped out of the van and joined the speaker as they both sprinted towards the turn of the road. The road here has a blindspot, she noticed before planning the protest. The security is weak here, as the road is around a turn where cars struggle to pass. If something happens here, at least a few seconds will be needed to respond. She hired an assassin as a backup plan, if she got arrested.

It's raining heavily. The night lights are flickering in the rain. A giant alarm noise had started to go off. An announcement is being heard over the microphones about a fugitive on the run. The police patrol cars are starting to stroll across the city roads. Everything is overflowing with the amalgamation of the rainwater and the colours caused by various lights. The helicopter is buzzing overhead. Not long before she's found. As they camouflage among a bunch of Book Burners gathered nearby, Stana looked at the assassin for the first time. The man was around late sixties, she was sure about it. He was breathing heavily, as he took out his phone from his pocket to do something.

"Thanks.", She whispered to him. He nodded, without looking up. "Sorry to ask", She said, "But... Why do you do this? Why... now?"

The man looked up to her, with a crooked smile on his face, "How do you think common people survive here in WorldStage? The Committee doesn't care for us, they didn't even want to accept that we exist. We have to do whatever that pays for that day. We save people who pay us. We kill people whose death pays us. And we do that till we're dead. It's a funny place... But you get it, or they wouldn't be posting your pictures up there."

He pointed to a tall building nearby. A large picture of her was being projected on the building, with the details of her below the image. The microphones announced her fugitive status. The man looked around. She was placing her collars up to hide her face, but a few Book Burners looked at her with an inquisitive expression. He turned to Stana, "Now, what?"

Another tall building was now having the man's picture projected. 'Scott Benson, 67, armed and dangerous', she read. Stana looked at Benson, "Now we run."

Worldstage

Neon Xity looks poetic in the night, with the darkness intermingling with lights of the streets and buildings. The chopper overhead and the fireworks celebrating the Book Burning Ceremony were enough distractions for Brennan from enjoying that. He sighed. There's a lot of work to be done today. There's no time to waste now.

"Have you completed sending in your projects, kiddo? Everything shuts off from tomorrow onwards...", Sam said from the rooftop door. Brennan turned around. He thought he was lonely at the terrace, taking in whatever is left of beauty in this wretched city. Sam's voice startled him. He answered, "I'm about to, dad."

Sam laughed, "Well, go on then. We have the holidays to relax and catch up. But you've to complete your work first, my boy!"

Brennan started to walk down the staircase. His office closed today, although some important papers have to be sent in by tonight. Sam had been pushing Brennan to spend the holidays with him this year. He finally reluctantly accepted, coming here today to stay with his father for a few days. Walking down the stairs, Brennan touched his pocket. The revolver is tucked in there. Father can't know about this...

How old was he when mom was arrested and killed by this police state? He can't remember. Mom was a rebel, a protester against The Committee and everything that is wrong in WorldStage. It was Dad, he knows now, who helped the police to catch mom. She was executed by the authorities of WorldStage, charged with high crimes against the nation. 'High crimes' - the phrase made him laugh with disgust. He was so young to know anything then. He was so young to even know her. But he knows in his heart - every protester loves this nation. That's why they fight. They fight to save the nation. They believe there is still a chance to come back from this nightmare.

Krista. That was her name. That's one of the few things he remembered about his mother. And the fact that she was the most courageous person he would ever meet. Her face is blurry is his memory now, but Brennan can feel her impact inside of him.

He tried to run away from home all his life. Moved out from here on the first chance he got. Returning to this place feels like a Gothic terror. But he always went with the flow. Working on a dead-end job, spending day to day life in monotony. He could sustain himself. And that's all he did. Brenan often thought he was spending life, not living it. Then again, WorldStage breeds ghosts. Dead people rule dead people. The living perish.

Sam was enjoying the cold breeze of the night-time. The weather is sublime today. He still takes the Subway train home, but he can easily afford a car. Sam had been a distinguished lawyer for The Committee since ages. The local cases of arrested protesters and miscreants are handled by him. He relished in making sure these thugs suffer for what they've done. WorldStage is a happy place, and none should even dare to disturb that peace here.

Sam breathed in. The smell of rain has felt sublime to him since he was a young boy. He looked on at the Neon Xity streets from the rooftop. He has aspirations. He has worked hard in his career. And it's about time he starts working at the national level. One-day, maybe, The Committee notices that he's a man made for higher purposes. One day he might be sitting at the top chairs of the nation. That's what he liked about WorldStage. It's a textbook example of a perfectly functioning system. If one works hard, one can reach any height.

If one is rich, ofcourse. But that is a given. Poor people are not allowed to dream. Everyone knows that.

The announcement in the microphones derailed his train of thought. Sam looked at the large buildings nearby, on which two huge pictures were being projected. A young lady around his son's age, and a veteran man. The announcements said they were fugitives, and were fleeing from the police. Everyone should be on alert, in case the criminals come to this city.

Sam concentrated on the announcements. The two thugs broke out of a prison van, killing five armed guards. Despite the extensive search, they've escaped from the police. It is being speculated that they hid among the Book Burners and eventually ran off through an under-construction tunnel. The incident happened in RedGarden Xity, and the police had issued a nationwide search for the two people. They are, Sam knew in his heart even before the microphones confirmed his theory, hardened dangerous terrorists who want the end of WorldStage's peaceful lifestyle.

Sam shook his head in irritation. These people would be dead in the streets in two days maximum. The police would hunt them down, for sure. There's no escape in WorldStage.

Revolution

"How do you even know this place?" She was out of breath, gasping for air. The tunnels run through the undergrounds of RedGarden Xity. Scott led her to one such tunnel, closed off because of construction work. An abandoned underground railway road. Since then they've been running. The police would be waiting on the other side of it. They could hear running sounds of heavy boots behind. Scott took Stana with him off to a detour, a road different from the one leading to the tunnel's other end. They reached a closed off doorway of the tunnel that opened up to a building. As they ran towards the building, Stana noticed the hovering helicopters overhead. Spotlights were being used to spot the fugitives. Avoiding the flashing lights and hiding in the shadows, the two reached the building. While trying to catch her breath, she asked, "How do you even know this place?"

The mercenary smiled, "In this job, one has to know things. This was supposed to be the office for the railroads. The project never came to fruition. They surveyed that this locality consists of mostly economically backwards people. People who can't even afford a railway route. So The Committee abandoned the project. The project could have changed the situation of this place, it could have improved the condition of the people here. But when has WorldStage thought about anyone other than its rich, right?"

Stana sat down on the ground, and leaned back on the wall of the dilapidated room. The building is full of wild plants and dust and trash. It's falling apart, she thought. Looking at Scott, she asked, "I reached out to you at random. I had to look for a mercenary for hire while avoiding the watchful eyes of the authority. I contacted a few people and were led to you. But why did you accept the job? You knew the WorldStage police would come at you with full force... Is this something you always do?"

While checking the magazine of his gun, Scott answered without looking at her, "The short answer is money. People are dying. We're dying. This job was the first offer in a while. And I needed to be able to eat. I've been doing this job for a while, so I know a thing or two about avoiding the police. Granted, they would be trying to capture us with all their might this time. But that's the fun, though. The scope of landing a few punches before getting taken out. Pointing out the chinks in their shining armour, you know?"

Stana laughed, "You are one of us, aren't you, Mr. Benson? A rebel?"

Scott put the bullets in another gun and handed it over to Stana, "I don't know. I have to live. And if they hired me to kill one of you, I would do so. But yeah, The Committee ruined us all. And they should pay for it, sooner rather than later."

Stana checked the rounds of the gun and kept it in her hand. For seven years, she had trained to use guns of different kinds. She has been preparing for a war all her life. Maybe it is here now. Stana spoke again, "Very well. So what do we do from here?"

Scott stood up, "We hide in the shadows. Lay low. Maybe cross city borders. And then we figure things out on the go. And one more thing-"

There was a slow footstep on the building, she could hear. The heavy boot almost silently stepped into the room, and she opened the gun's safety catch and pulled the trigger. The empty building echoed with the gunshot sound, as the dead policeman collapsed on the floor with a thud. Stana looked at Scott, "Don't hesitate to shoot? Is that what you were saying? I won't, Scott."

The building was overflowing with searchlights now, and numerous heavy boots could be heard. The choppers were coming down, the loud noise of those were deafening. Microphones were announcing to the Force that they should shoot to kill at the moment the terrorists were on sight. A few rogue firings shattered the already broken windows of the building. Scott took his position behind a wall, his gun ready in his hand, "Well then, let's go to war."

Home

The Subway platform was buzzing with people. Brennan tuned out the cacophony as he stepped out of the train into the station. The festival is still ongoing. The crowd was a result of that. People will be traveling to Kapitol everyday. He was getting bored at home, so just wanted to take a trip to a few blocks' distance. Tackling the incoming crowd, Brennan got out of the station and stepped in the busy roads of Neon Xity.

The posters were the first thing that caught his eyes. Humongous pictures of two individuals who were, as the signs warned, dangerous criminals. He read the names again, written in the block letters. Stana Mitovich and Scott Benson. Brennan started walking. The posters are everywhere. It's been three days since these two broke out of a prison van. Apparently they were even cornered in an abandoned railway office, but the two fought back and managed to run away. They've been in the air since then. Brennan smirked. Three days dodging the WorldStage armed forces? Fighting back and winning? That has got to be a record. A one of a kind thing that would hurt The Committee's all-powerful image.

And it has affected them already, he knew. He has seen dad back at home, getting increasingly tense over these days. Rebel protesters pop up every so often, and get put down very fast. Samuel Dartmoor had made a career out of being Neon Xity's poster child of bringing misery to these folks in a kangaroo court. The incident took place in RedGarden, so he doesn't have any jurisdiction there. But he had been making phone calls and talking with people all over the country. He's a small man with huge aspirations, Brennan realized this about his father a long time ago. Small men with huge aspirations are dangerous people. Dad has always been one.

Armed guards and overhead helicopters are things that he had known all his life. But even then, the tighter security seemed very apparent to him. The festival time usually sees a rise in security details, and the mishap with the fugitives had made the situation all the more tense.

How does anyone breathe in this wretched nightmare - he had been pondering all his life.

Brennan walked around aimlessly for a while. Agreeing to spend the holidays with dad was a bad idea. Should he go to his own apartment to relax on his own for a while? He dismissed the idea. The traffic would be tricky. He sat down at a roadside coffee shop. The Artificial Intelligence did a quick scan about his identity, whether he's carrying weapons and a few more things. Leaving the gun in his room - at dad's apartment - was a terrifyingly risky thing to do. But he had to do that before getting out. In the Subway or anywhere else, his weapon would be detected. And that would land him in a lot of trouble. He hid it well in his room. That was the less dangerous choice he could make between the two. Right now, he didn't have to be stressed about the scan. He knew there would be nothing suspicious found. After he was cleared, he typed in his order. As the beverage came, he sat there drinking the coffee and looked on at the road. Police. Book Burners. Posters of fugitives. This was home.

He sighed. When does it all end? How does this end? Brennan kept on looking at the giant screens all over the streets. The images alter between propaganda and the alert for the fugitives. The screens were showing images from the Kapitol now. The huge decorated statue of Iago, and thousands of people gathering and burning down books. He shivered inside, but knew how to control the expression outward. He had the chance to read. Sam was a loyalist of The Committee, So his son was allowed education. He knew the world through books, despite how censored the access was. It gave him a mind of his own. The ability to think for himself. The ability to see through this fascist regime's facades.

The screens switched back to the posters of the fugitives. A gust of wind made him chilly suddenly. He felt something like an epiphany. A storm was brewing. And it was bigger than them all. He could sense it, somehow.

Stranger

A stray black cat jumped out of the darkness suddenly and leapt onto the wall. Looking at her, he meowed. Stana laughed and put her hand forward, "Hey there, stranger!"

The cat brushed his head on her hand and purred. She gently patted it, "Good to meet you, gentleman. But hey, I have to go in now, OK? There's a lot of work to be done. We'll talk soon."

The cat looked at her eyes. She felt like he knew what she meant. The cat slowly turned back and started walking back to the darker corner from where he came out. That was his home, she guessed. Stana smiled and walked inside the house.

"Am I going insane or were you just talking to a cat?" Scott said, while putting their guns in a safe place. She laughed without saying anything. The room had a couch. Stana sat down and took a deep breath. Scott was still saying something. She couldn't concentrate. Stana closed her eyes. Everything went black. No sound. No images. The world was nonexistent. She opened her eyes again.

How long has it been that they're running from the WorldStage army? Nine days to be precise. The whole nation had been put on high alert. That day, she and Scott managed to escape from the building by an inch. It was a miracle, being able to hold off the regime's brutal force. Since then, they've managed to not come in contact with the police anymore. Hiding in the shadows had been challenging. The two had managed to find shelters in some citizens' houses once in a while. It was a terrifying thing to do, opening up their doors to the people WorldStage is hunting down. If the fugitives were found, they would be taken down too. But some people still came by their side.

Why were these people by their side? Stana didn't know exactly. WorldStage was an almost self-conscious sentient all-consuming monster which devoured anything that stood in its way, and even some who have been its enablers. People were sad, were broken, were terrified. But they - she thought - were not by her side because of the fear, but because of the courage. She and Scott just stared down the Devil on a few occasions, and in them these people might have found something grander. This was something far greater, Stana realized. This was the bell ringing of a change. She had an answer to give. An answer to destiny. Running away was not the answer. She knew, they had to stop running. And start fighting back.

Destiny came to her door with a proposition. And she was up for it.

While running from the forces of The Committee, she told Scott one day - "Hey, I've to say this. There's no point of return in this stage. I'm not gonna choose to either. Scott, The Committee needs to be taken down. We're in a cage, and we've been dying for so long. The time for revolution had come and gone. But it's a fight that I would see the end of. And I'm not gonna drag you into this. You were supposed to break me out. You did. The rest was not your duty. But you still did. But going up against The Committee directly is something way bigger deal. If you wanna call it quits, I understand. We'll manage on our own in our different paths."

Scott looked on at the horizon, as the setting sun was still beaming with a pride from yesteryear. He sighed, "I've been dead all my life. We've all been, in WorldStage. What's the cost of trying to be alive, huh? Worst case scenario, we come back to where we began. Their tortures can't hurt more than the life that they gave us hurts. Let's bring down hell on these monsters."

They've been growing in numbers. It was she and Scott, but a number of people joined them during these days. The group movement made it easier to camouflage in the crowd, or slip away when routine police searches took place. The two of them had some connections, and these people brought in resources with them. Crossing the RedGarden Xity border secretly was something she thought wouldn't be possible. But it was necessary. And they even managed to do that.

WorldStage was a rotten system. And it let its people rot. A system which ruins its people, brings with it crimes. Smuggling was rampant in the country, and The Committee took down anyone associated with it with ruthless brutality. It was a crisis they created, and then pretended to solve it to make themselves look like the helping hands. But hunger, like a bad habit, survives. This place won't look after the suffering citizens, so they had to make their own ways to survive. Smuggling still survived, despite the crackdown. There were tunnels through which it happened. Stana and Scott, and the people who joined them, used those routes to cross the border undetected.

Sitting on the couch, she could envision all those events infront of her eyes. They'd spend the night here. This place is close to the border they just crossed. It's risky, but traveling further tonight would have been trickier.

Scott came up to her, "Hey, so, I've put some of our weapons here. I'm going to the room which I've been given here. You take some rest now. Try to sleep. Our next step remains unchanged, right?"

She nodded, "Yes. Xity-Five Osmosis. G'night Scott."

"G'night." Scott walked out the door to the other room. She locked the chamber. The helicopters are making rounds in the sky, she could hear. Getting out of this room would be a death sentence at this moment. She couldn't sleep now, she knew.

Stana looked at the dark night outside the window. "You there, Mr. Cat?" She said in a hushed tone, "Stranger?"

With a meowing sound, the cat jumped inside the room through the window. Stana laughed, "You like the name? 'Stranger'? I'm gonna call you that then..."

The cat slowly walked towards her and climbed up on the couch. She laid back on the couch, and the cat sat by her side. Stana sighed, "So tell me something about you. Let's chat..."

The Lawyer

"**S**ure, Ma'am. I will be available as soon as possible."

Sam disconnected the video call. Looking outside the window, he felt a rush of emotions. His heart was full. He was happy.

The Book Burning Ceremony is still happening all-over the country. These people will be going to Kapitol Xity. And he, too, would be going there. But for a very different reason. He's not a very emotional person as such, but Sam felt his eyes were getting misty. The top brass of The Committee had called on to him. He just had a conversation with one of the highest post holders of the organization. She said that WorldStage is thankful to Samuel Dartmoor for his enormous contributions in safeguarding the country's integrity. He's, she said, someone for whom The Committee had high hopes. "One day, Mr. Dartmoor", the woman - Professor Robins was her name - said, "When the guards change hands and a new batch of staff comes in to take on this job, I can imagine you being here working with us directly. I don't think that day is very far, even. Keep working hard, Mr. Dartmoor. Hard work is always rewarded in WorldStage, as you know. These are the times of our lives."

That's the thing he respected the most about The Committee. Its transparency. It took care of WorldStage's rich people. Because that is the law of nature. That is how things should be. The rich take care of this place, and the place in return nourishes the rich. It's a healthy system that sustains the stability. Sustains the balance of nature. Sustains democracy. Preserving the wealthiest of the wealthy is, he had always believed, the only scientific approach in conducting how democracy should work. Equality for everyone was unnatural. One day, he knew deep in his heart, would the wealthiest only remain. That was the kind of equality WorldStage was slowly building towards. Eradicate the weak. And what were poor people, if not weak - he thought.

Professor Robins' words moved him. The fact that The Committee was not only recognising his efforts, but also encouraging him to keep on prospering, telling him they had faith in him - it was overwhelming for Sam. He had believed in The Committee all his life. And today, they said that they know he'd be able to sit on one of the highest chairs one day. What more can a humble man dream for in a lifetime? WorldStage gave everyone a chance to evolve. To sustain. To survive. He succeeded in it. That is how it is.

It has been nine days since the incident at RedGarden Xity. The fugitives had picked up a few followers on their way. The WorldStage armed forces announced this to be a full-fledged attempt at terrorizing the people of the nation. It's an attack on the humane basis of cohabitation and prosperous harmony on which the WorldStage civilization had been built upon. Sam was getting increasingly disturbed by this news. Spine, he knew, was a very bad thing. This young lady on the posters had clearly had one. The problem with people who have backbones is this - they inspire others to find their own confidence. People might start believing in themselves. Free will, Sam thought to himself, is something that he respected very much. It's a common human thing, and ofcourse The Committee won't take away people's freedom. The Committee is for the people at its core. He is for the people. But people need to trust the ruler more than they trusted themselves. "Everyone must keep their heads high", read the first line of the country's New and Codified Constitution, "But not higher than The Committee." His entire career was devoted to make sure heads stay where they belong. These two rebels and their followers were messing up the beautiful, peaceful equilibrium of WorldStage. He made a few contacts, conversed with few people, but couldn't do much. He didn't have a jurisdiction in RedGarden Xity, after all.

The news came to him earlier today. The rebels were spotted at the border. In Neon Xity, he cracked down on the smuggling racket. He has sources in other cities too. One such source gave him the information that the rebels were using tunnels to cross borders. It was tempting to give the news to the police. But Sam thought to check himself. The info might be false. And he couldn't put his reputation in jeopardy. If the information turned out to be fake, The Committee would never forgive him for wasting their money and resources. And

Sam knew how unforgiving The Committee can be. He had been the hand many times which delivered The Committee's verdict. Yes, he was a lawyer by profession. And yes, the people outside of this city might not know who he was, yet - but Sam knew that in Neon Xity court rooms, he was the true judge. He was the one who delivered the verdict, actually. And yet, he had never let pride take a hold of himself. He still worked hard, walked down rainy streets with an umbrella, and still used public vehicles. And the people respected him for that. It's a respect he couldn't put in danger.

So he waited. He wanted to confirm the news through other resources. And he knew, none's have anything to lose in this scenario. He wanted the fugitives to escape today. The WorldStage police would inevitably gun them down in a few days, but he might be the one who could end up causing that. If the news was true, and the fugitives escaped, he'd be able to present the info to The Committee - making a case for himself as a potential candidate for higher chairs. If he could be the one who led the police to the rebels, then that would definitely make him a person of interest for The Committee.

Sam was soon sure that the rebels were indeed at the border. He waited for further news to come regarding them moving on from there. When that came, he made contacts with The Committee. Sam said the news came after the terrorists had already escaped. He, Sam emphasized, merely did his work as a dutiful citizen who loves WorldStage. And he's deeply apologetic if he had broken any protocol by showing interest in the inner workings of another city jurisdiction. "The issue is not only a national issue", Sam expressed to JJ Williams - the member of The Committee to whom he talked, "But also, Sir, all of these cities, all of us are a family. We share now our problems, as much as we have shared our happiness all these years. There has never been anything remotely problematic here, before these goons created this crisis. Under the strong leadership of The Committee, Sir, I know, we'll be back to normal very soon."

"Your work is appreciated, Dartmoor", Williams replied, "But one little thing. There's nothing about going back to normal. Everything is normal. It's a problem that is being dealt with. And good citizens like you are actively helping us."

This conversation resulted in his call with Professor Robins. Robins said The Committee was highly appreciative of Sam's work, and would follow up on the lead. Further, the Chairs wanted to meet and have a conversation with him face to face. Sam accepted the invitation and said that he'd be at the Kapitol for the meeting as soon as he could. The Common Folks are not allowed to use the flights for intercity travels, so they travel via subway rails to go to the capital for The Book Burning Ceremony. Sam would be able to use a flight though. But everything comes to a halt during the Ceremony. He'd need to make a few calls.

Sam gets up from his table. He'd been in his study for a while now. Brennan must be getting bored. Who knew he'd get so busy during the holidays? His plans to spend time with Brennan were going off the rails.

Sam smiled to himself. He'd take Brennan to Kapitol with him. The kid's never been there. It'd be an experience for him. And they'd be able to catch up in-between Sam's working hours. That, he knew, was a solid plan.

Xity-Five Osmosis

Stana checked the gun before putting it in her pocket. It was full. Her backpack carried a few weapons. Scott had firearms with him, and this ever-growing team had provided some. Going to Xity-Five Osmosis would not be an easy job. These would be coming handy.

Going to that place was a collective decision. Osmosis Xity was an infamous place in WorldStage. It was a humongous city, largest in country. Almost four-time larger than the Kapitol. Osmosis Xity had always been a place that The Committee hated. The people there were always at odds with the forced inhuman rules that the organization put upon the common people. Protests against The Committee were constant. And WorldStage had always been eager to shush voices which don't echo its monotone. The armed guards brutalized Osmosis Xity, killing numerous people. And yet it couldn't break the spirit of those people. They could think on their own. And that terrified these powerful folks. It was largely believed an underground library still survived somewhere in Osmosis Xity, where people from even other cities went secretly to read. WorldStage police have tried to dig up the place many times, but still couldn't find it. People were the source of power there, to other people. And The Committee had figured out that already. The entire city had been broken down in seven pieces, with each city named Xity-One Osmosis, Xity-Two Osmosis, and so forth. It was a brilliant and ruthless move which thwarted the rebellion. Cross-border journey to those seven cities had been prohibited, and The Committee had implemented strong rationing regulations that caused humongous crises there. Famine. Disease. Death. Osmosis was cut off from the rest of WorldStage, which itself was effectively secluded from the rest of the globe. Everything that happened in WorldStage, was kept in. It was home, afterall. And family matters, Stana remembered how the propaganda machinery had announced, are discussed inside the family only.

Courage is still such a thing that survives the toughest of challenges. The Committee effectively ruined Osmosis Xity, but scattered protests and rebellious efforts would raise their heads once in a while. Those would be flattened out fast with a flying helicopter dropping a bomb or something like that, but the willpower was visible. One city in particular, Xity-Five Osmosis, had continuously tried to fight back. It's a thing that was largely kept off the news, because that would hamper the propaganda of how everything was always smoothly working on WorldStage. How everything was full of happiness. How everything was bright and shiny here. Xity-Five is where they needed to be at, Stana and Scott discussed between themselves. There would be ammunition. There would be people who had the guts to take on the monsters of WorldStage. They needed a grander scheme. More people, more resources, more everything. Xity-Five could provide that.

There was still darkness when they left the house where the group stayed in the night, near the border. The police would be looking for them everywhere. Someone would have surely made the discovery that they've used the tunnels to cross borders. This was the second time they did so, after the initial faceoff with the police in RedGarden Xity. The police would be closing off all those underground roads for sure. They had to be on their feet, hiding in the shadows, stealing a vehicle when they could. There's no way they won't be facing the police in-between. Stana breathed in, standing at the outside of the house at the crack of dawn. They would need to fight through the minions of The Committee. She was cool with it. This was war. As it should be.

Scott came up, "Morning, leader. We are all packed up and ready to go. Let's proceed then?"

Stana raised an eyebrow, laughing, "Leader?" Scott nodded, "Yep. That's the truth, chief. So, what do we do now?"

She cracked her knuckles, "Now we give them hell." Scott smiled and walked on. Stana pushed her hair back. Morning looked so poetic now. There's hope still left in this wretched mess. There's life left.

Something brushed on her legs. She looked down. The stray black cat was sitting there and purring. "Hey, Stranger!", Stana said softly, "Morning. It was good to meet ya. We're leaving now. Stay well, good sir."

The cat looked at her for a few seconds, his paws gently put over her foot. He meowed again. Stana smiled, "You wanna join us folks? You want to come with me?"

The cat meowed again. Stana sat down by the cat, "Yah? Come on then, Stranger. We don't wanna waste time, do we?"

The cat jumped on her shoulders and stayed there comfortably as she stood up and started walking. "Good boy", the rebel smiled as brightly as the morning sun that was about to come up.

Kapitol

The statue was way larger than he always thought it to be.

Brennan was standing in front of the Iago monument, amongst the other festival enthusiasts. It's been over a week that he has stayed in Kapitol now. Coming here was not his decision, and he was not even remotely interested to join his father when Sam made the proposal. The Book Burners would gather here in numbers, and that's an imagery right out of a nightmare. But Brennan had never been to Kapitol, and part of him wanted to visit the place. What Sam was up to, he had a hint of that. And that terrified him. Nevertheless, he knew that dad would be busy with his work, and for the most part he'd be left to himself. He liked that. That would give him the time to explore the city. Visiting the Book Burners' gathering was a way to look into the heart of darkness. Brennan wanted to stare at the abyss and waited to see if it stared back, or blinked. It's a bottomless pit in which WorldStage people had been falling into, since forever. Where is the landing, afterall, he wanted to see for himself increasingly, everyday.

One week. One week in Kapitol had been busy for Sam, Brennan presumed. Dad's attempt to spend time with him got botched because of the rebels. Although Sam never talked about his office work with anyone else, Brennan picked up on a thing or two through overheard phone calls and such. Sam had gathered some intel on the fugitives, and The Committee wanted to see him regarding that matter. Since coming here, one thing has been made public by the WorldStage authorities. The rebels had somehow managed to cross the RedGarden Xity border. That, Brennan thought, was absolutely impressive. Making the info public would be hurting The Committee's reputation, but they had to issue a formal announcement which asked the public to tip the organization if they had any info on the fugitives. The notion made Brennan chuckle. The all-powerful Committee wants people's help? A handful of rebels did that to them? What would happen - what can happen - if the entire country stood up against these monsters?

The posters everywhere and digital screens flashed the information about these people all the time. Minute details about the rebels had been pointed out in order to help the common folks identify them in a crowd. The rebels have gotten out of RedGarden, and might be anywhere. One little bit of information made Brennan chuckle amidst all these. Apparently a black cat had been seen with the fugitives. It's been pointed out in the announcement as a marker to identify the group if they're hiding in plain sight. A cat joining the rebellion, Brennan thought, was the coolest thing he's ever heard.

He came to the statue today. The celebration of a monolithic institution. Face of the rule of propaganda. How are so many people swept up in this frenzy? Why is everyone so eager to publicly bend the knee to the people who torment them? These Book Burners - they all do these things to show their loyalty to The Committee. Is that only fear? Or something else? He's read in one of the books how the mass frenzy leads people to go with the flow, how the people want to be by the side of the potential winners. Is that how The Committee succeeds? He didn't have a clear answer. All he knew was that this binding spell on people by the authorities of WorldStage had to be broken. Can these rebels do that? Looking on at the statue, Brennan sighed. Can things change, or is it too late already? Has the monster won once and for all, and they quite never figured it out...?

"Orwell is dead", the crowd chanted together, "We've killed him." There was a humongous basket in front of the statue. The incoming crowd had been dropping books in them since morning. With a round of applause, the armed guards ignited the fire in the basket. The books went up in flames. "I am not what I am", the plaque with Iago's words were beaming with the light that came from the fire. The crowd was screaming and clapping. Brennan felt nauseous, it seemed he would throw up. Running away would attract attention, so he slowly turned away and started walking.

These comparative small scale burnings would take place everyday, leading up to the final day, when thousands and thousands of books are set on fire with grand display. The fire, he had heard since childhood, can be seen from everywhere in Kapitol. That is how much it burns. WorldStage eradicated education for the masses, so these books are basically the magazines and pulp fictions which The

Committee believes to be harmless enough to not censor or ban. These are old prints from a different era, now nothing new is printed for the public other than propaganda. These books remained with people over generations or so. The masses are encouraged to burn them down during the festival by The Committee, as it is - according to them - a statement. A statement regarding what, Brennan always wondered. What is the statement in burning down literal knowledge or banning and censoring it? This was a celebration of a fascist rhetoric.

Brennan kept on walking, his hands kept in his overcoat pocket. He'd have felt comfortable if he could feel the gun there, but it had to be kept at the hotel again. To carry a weapon in a different city would have been impossible, but Brennan didn't have to go through checking procedures due to Sam's position as a Committee loyalist. A private plane dropped them here. But in the city, when he was on his own, he couldn't afford to carry that gun. The security is tighter than it was mere days ago. WorldStage, Brennan realized with a dark amusement, had found itself in a weird jeopardy. The festivity causes a relaxation of the rigid proceedings of the nation. Lot of things are closed. Way too many people everywhere. These things, he could understand, were helping the fugitives to stay hidden and make movements. But The Committee couldn't outright cancel the festivity, or open up the closed offices etc. That would be an acceptance of the fugitives' capabilities, a straightforward presentation of their impact. WorldStage can't do that. The Committee had to swallow the bitter pill. Everything is going on as it is, and thus the pretension of normalcy had stayed intact. Knowing full well how these are essentially helping the rebels, the organization had to go forward with these proceedings. Small victories then, Brennan smirked as he crossed the road, small victories. If he can see through this shenanigan, surely other people can too. Surely they are also starting to see the chinks in the armour of The Committee? The realisation should be dawning that the organisation is not as powerful as it likes to pretend...

The screens in front of him flashed the pictures of the rebels. He kept walking. The police were tearing off something from the wall. Brennan glanced quickly. A poster of the rebel called Stana, over which someone spray painted the word "FAITH". Brennan murmured to himself under his breath, "Stay the hell away from them, Dad."

The Committee

The weather was chilly here. A bit of drizzling could be seen through the huge glass windows. Sam was standing at the balcony of this office space, and looking out. This is a branch office of The Committee. His meeting with the higher ups had taken place here. And for a week, he'd been coming to this place, hoping for some good news. But nothing of that sort has happened. The fugitives are still in the air. Things have only gotten worse.

The Kapitol journey was important for him. It had the potential to launch him in the national stage. The first day of coming here, Sam got to meet the higher ups of the organization here face-to-face for the first time. He was congratulated for his efforts. Sam was standing there, in the huge hall in front of the very people whom he had idolized his entire life. These are the hands that keep the machine of The Committee running. These are the people who help WorldStage restore the natural balance of the society. They deserved utmost respect. And Sam was vocal in conveying those feelings. He was professional, putting his words immaculately. Emotions shouldn't get the better of oneself, he had known that always. Compliments shouldn't sound like being an yesman. He was not one. The Committee wouldn't like that, either. It gives the citizens proper respect, and expects to receive the same in return. They honoured the people of WorldStage, and The Committee deserved - rightly - to be honoured. A fare exchange of gratitude that went both ways. This organization had been built upon the basis of human rights and the notion that everyone can evolve. The Committee worked hard to create a culture in WorldStage that created people to strive to become their best versions through honest means. There was no corruption here. And so, The Committee hated sycophants. It didn't need them. The machine which provided peace for all needed hard workers, not brainless minions. Sam knew that. And this ideology of the organization made him respect them even more. He was never a yesman. And so he put it very professionally how much pride he takes to be recognised by the most important people of WorldStage, and how he looked forward to be able to contribute even more in the organization's continuous effort to take the nation to even greater heights.

The Committee members were appreciative. From them, Sam got to know some additional information about the fugitives. His info helped the police to track down the terrorists. There had been a huge altercation between them and WorldStage forces. The fugitives had more ammunition than expected. They've managed to escape capture again, and neither any of them nor any of the forces of The Committee had lost their lives. "This", Sam was told, "is being kept out of the news, Mr. Dartmoor. You are a thinking man, you can realize telling this to the masses would make them irrationally stressed over a trivial matter. And to do that to the citizens - and in WorldStage, we're all family here - during a festival is something we can't do. You get what we are saying?"

Sam knew loud and clear what he was being told. The failure of The Committee to bring in the fugitives again was classified information. And if he somehow slipped up and the news reached anyone else, then things would become difficult for him. Sam was not intimidated by the realization. It was not a threat, afterall. It was diplomacy. Safeguarding of a well-functioning mechanism is necessary. The lawyer sharply nodded, "I do understand. Thank you for trusting me with the details."

"We're all family Mr. Dartmoor", Sam was told in return, "Trust is the main thing which makes WorldStage the greatest place to be in the entire Earth."

His impeccable work in Neon Xity spoke for itself, and Sam was asked to join the investigating members in a few meetings, regarding the fugitives. The past week had been spent in that regard. The Committee was in the trail of the rebels. But not admitting that they've been putting up a fight to the masses was leading to a weird jeopardy. The Committee could not bring out full forces to battle the fugitives from running. It would make a spectacle, which would be an open acceptance that they were now facing a full-blown uprising. Over the week, the fugitives and the armed forces had gone toe-to-toe, and both sides lost members to the bullets. To Sam's irritation, neither Ms. Mitovich nor Mr. Benson had been gunned down. The Committee even considered dropping overhead bombs, but members within the organization argued against it. What was done in Osmosis Xity was not easy to repeat in other places, especially during the festival season when numerous people were gathered everywhere. The death toll would be too much to write it off as collateral damage. That would dent the image of The Committee as the organization which loved everyone. "And", they said, "that image is the truth. That is The Committee, a mechanism that merely works according to the people's will." Sam had to agree. What the rich thought of The Committee, didn't matter much in reality. But making them go against the organization based on false information might stop the smooth working of WorldStage, which is the utmost necessity for the well-being of the citizens. Despite these altercations, the fugitives seemed to grow in numbers, signifying that they were being joined by new people every single day. People were being brainwashed by these rebels into believing a false cause. A bombstrike might give everyone - even the comfortable wealthy community that is not affected by this whole ordeal at all - a chance to stop and introspect. People, Sam knew, should not be given a chance to be able to look within themselves. People shouldn't think. At all.

The forces stayed in the trail till yesterday, but then the fugitives had managed to lose them. A week later, The Committee were back to where it started, before Sam tracked the rebels down. They were in the air, and none had any idea where they could be.

Sam was standing in the balcony, looking at the rain. The posters could be seen from here, digitally projected in the tall buildings outside. The glass and the rain made the image unclear, but Sam still could figure out it was of Ms. Mitovich. Where is she? Sam thought to himself. Mr. Benson and she started this whole thing, but she's clearly the one leading the project. But what is the project, at the end of the day? What's the next step? Sam looked on at the posters. It's not merely interesting how these folks had managed to vanish. These are old tricks. They ran, that's the basic thing. They managed to escape from the forces. But where are they going? And how far are these people willing to go?

Sam started to walk towards the lift. He had been asked to go home for today. His prospect for a future, Sam understood, was not looking that bright now. The Committee valued him for his resources. His resources resulted in nothing after all. If this whole thing backfired, The Committee would need a scapegoat. Someone who'd be blamed for the fiasco. He might be labeled as a traitor, who was helping the fugitives. This is how the system works, Sam knew. He had orchestrated things like this before. "Full circle?", Sam murmured to himself, and then swiftly got a hold on his psyche.

Pressing the button of the lift, Sam stood silently on the crowded chamber of the elevator. The rebels would be brought back. There's no revolution coming. There had never been one. And there won't be any in the future, either.

Alliance

Stana knocked on his door, "How are ya holding up there?"

Scott moved his hand to signal her to come in. His other hand was wrapped in a bandage, a sign of the scuffle with the police force. Stana was also injured, her left leg took a hit. There was a scar on her forehead. The mercenary smiled, "Not gonna die till we give it back to these demons what they have had coming for years now."

He was sitting on the ground, Stana sat down there by his side. She sighed, "You're not gonna die on me, Scott, we're in this together, right?"

The mercenary nodded, "Yah... yah." She sighed, "All these people died, Scott, because of us. They joined us hoping for a change. We dragged them into this war, and the police gunned them down. What do I do with this blood on my hands? How do I move forward now..."

Her thoughts trailed off, and the rebel fell silent. Scott was out of words too. Those were legitimate questions which Stana was asking. The two of them started this. They're the people on whom these people have put their faith. One can prepare their mind thinking sacrifices had to be made when a battle comes knocking, but to experience it felt different. He had killed for money, as that was a way of survival. There had been blood on his hands for a long time. But this... this felt different. How does he go on with that? He didn't know. He didn't know either.

Another knock on the door. Both of them looked up. Another member of their group was standing, "The people of Osmosis have come with the car."

Stana stood up, "Hey, Scott, I can do this on my own. Shouldn't you take rest?" Scott smiled, "Chief, you are way more injured than I am. I saw you take on The Committee's forces over this week. You don't need me, I know. But I need to be by your side."

The mercenary was struggling to get up. Stana extended her hand. As he stood up holding her hand, Stana hugged Scott, "I'm always gonna need you, my friend."

They walked out of the house and into the dark, silent roads of Xity-Five Osmosis. The car was waiting. Stana took a step towards the car, and then halted as she heard a purring noise. Without even looking back, she laughed, "You too don't wanna rest then, Stranger? Come along then." The cat jumped on her shoulder. Scott and she got into the car. The vehicle geared up and soon vanished into the night.

The breeze was touching her face, messing up her hair. The cat leapt down on the seat and made himself comfortable. Stana was looking outside. Two days ago, they managed to brush off the armed forces of WorldStage from their trails. That was important. If the police figured out that they were venturing towards Osmosis Xity, it would have been a catastrophic damage to their course of action. They reached Xity-Five two days ago. And the conversations with the rebel forces here had been going on since then. Stana and Scott sat down with them to lay out a plan. People from here had been really helpful to visualize the grand scheme that she wanted to make the landing stick. The people of Xity-Five had agreed to join the battle. They'd be providing ammonunitions, and resources. They'd been kept at the periphery for so long, the citizens told Stana. WorldStage tried to erase Osmosis Xity from the face of the Earth. And in turn, The Committee had forgotten that it still has power. The Committee obliterated any effort of rebellion, but this was the moment. They made Stana and Scott an offer. They'd be by her side. But only Xity-Five can't do it. The power of Osmosis Xity lay in its people. People who had been scattered. They asked help to bring in people from the other broken down six parts of the former Osmosis Xity. "We've the resources", they told Stana, "You people have the expertise of crossing borders and avoiding the WorldStage police. Let's bring in more people together. More hands. More guns. More ideas."

Stana had to think for a while. She came here for help. What's the point if these people are depending on her in return? How're they gonna help her then? As the car took hidden discreet roads to take her and Scott to the rebel leaders of Xity-Five, Stana found herself pondering over that thought. She would have to give an answer regarding that proposition today. She, Scott, and the others had a discussion. And they had agreed to help out the citizens of Osmosis Xity. If one thing that The Committee had done successfully, it is to eradicate human sympathy once and for all. This was a chance to help out each other. Tactically too, more people would be helpful in what they have in mind. What they need to do can't be done with a handful of people. This was a war for the soul of WorldStage. And it can't be won without an army. They needed to build that army up.

The car stopped. It was a discreet location, one of those rebel frontiers that still had managed to survive despite the attacks and bombings by the WorldStage armed forces. Stana and Scott walked inside the place. The rebels of Xity-Five were there. After greeting each other, Stana let them know that she's accepting the offer. "We need to start planning for the eventual and final step then", She said, "After the people safely reach to Xity-Five."

"Yes", a leader of Xity-Five rebels told Stana, "That is why we are here. The equipment etc. are all available here. Everything we would need to create a blueprint of our future endeavours. Come with me."

The woman took Stana to another room. There was a hatch in the room, and as the lady opened it, Stana could see a stairway that went under the ground. "What is this place?" She asked. The woman smiled, "Go ahead."

Stana took the stairs and went down the path. The lady followed her. Neon lights had been flickering in the route, and suddenly it opened up in a blinding white light. It took her a while to adjust her eyes, and then she stepped inside a room.

Stana looked around, her eyes wide. This was a gigantic room, full of cases with books. Thousands and thousands of books stacked in the bookcases, all around the room. People are reading, some are working with the gadgets, some are writing down in their devices and notebooks. Stana murmured almost involuntarily, "This... is.. the library."

The lady behind her laughed, "Yes, this is the place which The Committee had tried and failed to find. There are other rooms here. Our weapons are stacked there. Everything you need for the plan to succeed - from knowledge to ammunition - you'll find them here."

Stana looked around, and breathed in. This is the place from which the change would begin. As it should. She cracked her knuckles. They have long hours of work ahead. The Book Burning Ceremony ends in a few days. The Committee headquarter remains busy that day. It would be an act of statement. On the final day of the festivity, they would arrive on the Kapitol. Taking over the headquarters would be the first necessary step. It would be a tremendous battle, even if they succeed in the takeover. The Committee is a gigantic beast, taking them out from an office - or even a city - would do nothing. That is from where the war would need to begin in every city, in every part of WorldStage.

Stana looked at the woman, "Let's get to work then."

War

The microphones all over the city were making the announcements, "Red alert! Red alert! Citizens are requested to stay inside. The terrorists have attacked the Kapitol. Stay inside."

The Iago statue was glowing in the morning sun. The streets of Kapitol Xity were full of bullets and deaths. The war was here.

"Boom!" Scott heard the thundering sound and saw part of the building that he was in collapse. Three armed officers were running in, guns blazing. Scott hid behind a wall and aimed his rifle. Bang! Bang! Bang! There were no sound of the heavy boots now. Scott turned back to see other rebels holding off the forces. "Let's move, people!" Scott shouted, "Death to the dictators!"

"Death to the dictators!" The rebels shouted back. "Come on, now!" Scott threw a smoke bomb at the incoming force, and kept running with the team.

They were here. The day was finally here. The whole of Kapitol Xity had turned into a warzone. Scott could see the rebels taking on the police force all over the place. This was happening all around the city. The citizens of Osmosis Xity had taken control of the borders, taking out the patrol guards. They were holding off forces from outside the city from entering the Kapitol. WorldStage forces had to go airstrike mode, or fight in the streets. Scott knew they couldn't pull off a grander airstrike like they did in Osmosis. Fighting rebels can't lead to bombing their own citizens. Not that WorldStage cared, but it's a front they needed to put up. The collapsed building behind him was a stark reminder that small scale airstrikes were still a prospect that they needed to be aware of.

Scott was leading the rebel army through the roads. His hand was bleeding, he had to drag his leg which was severely injured. The plan had been executed right as it was drawn up. People from all over Osmosis Xity gathered in Xity-Five. From there, they arrived at

Kapitol border, and took on the forces head on. The Subway tracks were taken over, as it helped the rebels to move around the city fast and undetected. Systems were hacked, and online connective facilities were brought to a halt. The rebels were taking over the vehicles of WorldStage Police, and their ammunition. The guns and bombs were roaring all over the city, with the rebels and armed forces of The Committee facing off.

The chopper was flying overhead still, Scott could see. He looked around in the sky. There it was. Another helicopter was around. Someone was flying it. Another rebel was sitting by the door, facing the high force of the air. The rebel pointed the gun at the other chopper. The gun had been seized from the armed forces. The rebel pulled the trigger. The bombing chopper lost control and crash landed on the empty building it just bombed a few minutes ago, setting the whole thing on fire. Putting the gun down, Stana closed the copter door. A gun that can take out a humongous flying machinery. None should have that much power, let alone a ruthless organization like The Committee.

A few copters were at standstill in the police stations when they attacked, and they had taken those in. The rebels were firing from the sky and ground. The whole squad was moving towards The Headquarters, very near the statue.

"What's the news, Scott?" Stana asked via her device. The mercenary replied, "Moving in chief. Your team with the copters will be reaching first. We're coming in, Stana. Give them hell."

The security at The Headquarters was soon breached. Although The Committee had been evacuating, some members were still inside the building. The rebels wanted to have some people inside of the place. The Headquarters, Stana knew, would be a comparatively safe place with members of The Committee inside. Airstrikes or direct attacks couldn't happen if they had hostages.

With a deafening sound of a bomb, the door of The Headquarters blew open. The glasses shattered all around, and with a loud thud and cracking - the way inside the headquarters opened up. "That, my friend", Stana said as she gunned down the armed forces of The Committee waiting inside, "is the sound of revolution." The rebels were all over the building, guns blazing. "Death to dictatorship!" Someone shouted. "Death to dictatorship!" The others shouted back.

"I'm inside Scott", Stana was telling the mercenary, a few moments later. "We are near", he replied, " Will get in soon."

Stana looked around. This is the place from where The Committee ruled the people. "No more", she said to herself, "No more." There are a few secondary offices of The Committee in this city, the rebels had already got control over those. She was standing in the hall, with all the members of The Committee being put there in handcuffs. The rebels were guarding them.

"These are all the people who were here?" She asked. A member of the rebel army replied, "Yes, we've gone through this entire place."

Stana nodded, "Very well. Stay put. Avoid being in front of a window. They would be using snipers. Cover the gates, none of the WorldStage forces should be able to get in here. I'm going to the control room. We will be needing to start the broadcast soon."

Stana stepped out and started walking towards the stairs. Bam! A bullet from the outside shattered the glasses. Stana crawled down and fired back. And then kept crawling till she was out of the window's view. She was finally at the stairs. The rebels were using the elevators to move weapons and equipment, and that needed to happen smoothly. Stairway was the best option.

Stana reached the top floor. Control room. The room was being guarded by two rebel fighters. They nodded to her. Stana nodded back and entered the room.

The huge room was full of equipment and devices. There were no windows and it was built to be noise-canceling - no sound from inside the room went out, and nothing from the outside could come in. That was expected, Stana thought. This is the place from where The Committee broadcasts their propaganda. A bit of secrecy was the bare minimum. Presently, she was just thankful about the absence of windows.

Stana was looking around the room. She heard a subtle sound of movement and turned back with her gun pointed. A man in a suit was standing opposite her, with a gun in his hand sharply pointed towards her. Stana's jaws stiffened. Ofcourse, a room like this would have a secret compartment or something. The guy must have hidden there and avoided the rebels when they were searching.

The man spoke up, "It's nice to meet you face-to-face, Ms. Mitovich. I'm a lawyer. My name's Samuel Dartmoor."

IAGO

How far along was Scott? Would the rebels guarding this room be able to figure out something is wrong? The revolution was bigger than her, and she was a mere soldier in this movement. If she fell, that wouldn't impact the proceedings in any way. Her teammates would be able to carry it forward. The Committee would fall, one way or the other.

All of these thoughts came to her mind, like a stream of consciousness. Stana calmly replied, "Good afternoon, Mr. Dartmoor. You're a lawyer you said, so you're an appointee of The Committee. I don't believe in your ideologies. Come with me, and you'll be kept safe with your colleagues. I'm not interested in killing you."

"The thing is", Sam said, "I don't believe in negotiating with the terrorists, Ms. Mitovich. This was a happy place. It has forever been a happy place. And all of you ruined it."

Stana laughed, "We ruined it? Have you ever looked outside of your own comfort zone, Mr. Dartmoor? Do you know how many people die every year in famine in this nation? WorldStage cared about its wealthy only. And in return you people have given them your spines, your ability to think. The Committee doesn't care about you, Sam. It cares about surviving itself. You help it survive, so it sustains you. In a few years, WorldStage would even outgrow you. What then, huh, Sam? What then? Would people like you ever realize that problems exist when those are not directly affecting you?"

"That's the law of nature Stana", Sam replied to the rebel, "That's how science works. Survival of the fittest. This nation has evolved into the perfect system. And the perfect system doesn't work with the weak. With the poor. Wealth is literally the only currency in the modern evolved world. Empathy for the undeserving is unscientific, immature, unrealistic. Those are concepts from a bygone era. This is the new world where we live. This is utopia."

Stana looked Sam in the eye, "You people are gone so far off that there's no coming back. Very well. So be it. What now, Sam? I don't care if you gun me down. The revolution is bigger than me. It would outlive me. Or both of us, if it comes to that. Killing me is not gonna help you personally, nor would it help The Committee in a grander way. What do we do now, then? Come with me, and this might end with a lot less blood."

The lawyer moved his head sideways, "Yah. That's not gonna happen. We don't negotiate with terrorists here. And you are the face of this misguided attempt at a revolution. The Committee would stop this, for sure. And if you are out of the picture early due to me, The Committee might gain back some faith in me that they lost. The only reason I haven't pulled the trigger yet is because I need you to get out of this room safely."

Stana laughed, "Still trying to appease The Committee, Sam? You're in denial. Your world order has collapsed. Wake up and smell the coffee Sam. You're not gonna walk away from this. The revolution is here. And if it has to go this way, let's just get over with it."

With a cranking noise, a door opened in the room. Stana thought it was a wall before, but now as it opened up, she realized this was the doorway to the secret room inside. Neither she nor Sam moved an inch from their positions, but she noticed Sam's expressions change. A young man came out of the room and stood behind Sam, "Dad-"

Sam said somewhat irritatedly, "Brennan, go inside the room and stay there - as I said."

Stana didn't move her eyes from Sam at all. Her gun fixated on the man, finger on the trigger. Brennan spoke up again, his voice was a weird mix of calm, sure, confident and trembling - "Dad! Let her go!"

"What-?" Sam sounded like he was only mildly puzzled. He was a man who was failing to grasp the complete gravity of the situation, of the words that he just heard. Brennan spoke up again, "Let her go, Dad!" And with saying that, he took out the gun from his pocket and opened its safety catch.

Stana looked straight at Sam. Her gun didn't move. Her eyes didn't move. What was happening, she had no idea. She was trying not to think too much right now. Focus from the enemy shouldn't be distracted. Right this moment, it was clear who that was. A distraction might lead her ending up with a bullet, who knows from whom. She kept her mind clear. She was ready for everything. Right now, she needed to let this thing play out.

Without moving his eyes from Stana, Sam could hear the click of the safety catch removal. "You have a gun?" Sam's voice seemed like a different person to his own ears. Was he surprised? He was thinking too many things at once, trains of thoughts were losing track. Sam spoke again, "What the hell is up with you? Brennan, you're a kid. Stop this. Get back inside."

Brennan breathed in. He put his fingers steadily on the trigger, "Let. Her. Go. It's over Dad. The Committee's reign of terror is over. It's a new day."

"You're mistaken, son. You'll see", Sam's finger made a slight movement on the trigger.

'BANG! BANG!'

Before Sam could pull the trigger, the two different guns pointed towards him fired almost simultaneously. Samuel Dartmoor collapsed on the glass table and took it with him to the ground. With a loud noise, the glass shattered into innumerable pieces.

Stana immediately pointed her gun towards Brennan. Brennan was not looking at her. He was not looking at anything particularly. He fell on his knees and dropped the gun. Stana kept her gun pointed at him. After a few seconds, the man rose and walked towards Sam. Like a ghost, he stumbled through the room and came by the side of his father. Sam's lifeless body was collapsed amidst the broken glasses. Brennan looked on at him. Father was finally dead. As he should have been, a long time ago.

Stana picked up the other gun and put it in her pocket. She walked towards Brennan, "Hey, you're gonna be okay."

Brennan stood up, "I know. I know."

Stana looked at him, "Come on, let's get out of here. You wanna stay with me for now?"

He smiled, "Yah. Yah. That seems like a plausible option. And hey, keep the gun. I don't need it anymore. I'm not gonna try to kill you. He came here today for some work. Dragged me with him to show me the headquarters. They don't scan the loyalists or people who are with them. That's why I got to keep the weapon with me. When you people came knocking, he hid here with me. But yah, I don't need it anymore. I'm not gonna try to kill you."

The rebel smiled, "I know. I know. Now, let's go."

Stana opened the room's door to the surprised faces of the fellow fighters. She nodded, "I know. Will tell you later. Is Scott here?" The rebels nodded.

She was talking with Scott, a few moments later. Scott sighed, "You're not gonna die on me before all of this is over. Promises can't be one-sided."

Stanna hugged him, and Scott hugged the rebel back, "The change is here, Stana. I can feel it."

"Yah." She said. Scott looked at the outside, "But we need to block this road ahead. There are buildings and stuff behind the headquarters, and they can't bomb their own members. The police can't reach us through any of those two ways. The front. We need to block the front somehow."

Brennan was sitting closely. He was not sure what he was thinking, what he was feeling. He overheard the mercenary and walked towards them, "Sorry for intruding, but I think there's one way to block the roads."

The mercenary looked at him. Brennan said what he was thinking. Scott looked at Stana, "The guy's got a point, though! Should we try it?"

Stana thought for a while, and nodded, "Why not!"

She picked up the huge gun that was used earlier to take down the chopper, and extended it to Brennan, "They'd shoot if you're at the window. Don't die."

"I'm in no hurry", Brennan took the gun and walked up the stairs. He was on the third floor, waiting by the side of the window. The huge statue of Iago was just in front of The Headquarters, and can be seen through the window. Brennan picked up the gun, stood up in front of the window and pressed the trigger.

With a thundering noise, the humongous statue collapsed on the road and started burning. The armed forces of The Committee were shooting from the outside to the window. But hiding behind the wall, he could see the fire burning the statue and the plaque by its side. The road was now completely blocked.

Stana saw the statue collapsing on the road, and turned to Scott, "We need to hold off the forces. I'll try to make contacts. And then we'll broadcast." Scott nodded in affirmation.

It was burning so much, and so bright that probably it could be seen from everywhere in Kapitol. Brennan uttered under his breath, "Orwell lives, Mom."

People

The huge buildings all over the Kapitol were being projected with a live video. It was being broadcast from The Headquarters. The giant buildings were projecting the clip of Stana, standing in the room, and speaking to the people.

"This, fellow citizens of WorldStage", She said, "Is the new dawn. We've taken control of the place from where The Committee had decided the fate of each of our lives. This is from where The Committee cut us off from each other, and from the world. From here, we will begin fighting back. At this moment, we are contacting the outer civilized world, from which The Committee had kept their horrific acts hidden. The world from which they have kept us, and our sufferings, hidden. What happened in WorldStage, stayed at WorldStage. That won't be the deal anymore. We're making contacts with countries from all over the world. We've made contacts with the global organizations that had been established to make sure no human rights violation happens anywhere. The world now knows what a humanitarian crisis has been taking place here for more than a century now. Help is coming soon. Stay inside, stay safe my friends. The Committee had fallen. It can't hurt you anymore."

There were planes and helicopters landing all over WorldStage in the next hours. Rescue missions were being organized by countries and institutes from around the world. WorldStage was free now. Stana was standing in the middle of the little lawn outside the headquarters building. It was sunny today. The breeze is soft. She felt nice. "Stranger!" She called in a soft tone, and the cat came running from the building. "Good boy!", She said, and he jumped on her shoulder and stayed there perfectly. The huge screens all over the city were showing her, as well as the screens all-over the world by the news media who had arrived in WorldStage from all around the globe. The screens were showing the rebel. She was standing tall. Bleeding, but fearless. Gun in her hand, and a black cat comfortably sitting on her shoulder.

Brennan sat on the ground on the lawn and looked at the sky. He was feeling so many things, and he didn't know how to express them. Or how to even understand them. Maybe someday he will. Maybe someday...

Scott walked up to Stana, "Well." She looked back at him and smiled, "Well." Scott laughed, "Here we are." Stana nodded, "And we didn't die on each other before this was over."

The mercenary hugged the rebel again, and she hugged him back. The international armed forces were dropping in WorldStage, as an attempt to restore the law and help out the people of the nation regarding their essential needs. Looking at them, Scott said, "You do know right that we're gonna be picked up by the global authorities for all these?"

Stana laughed out loud, "Haha! I do know that, Scott, I do know that. And that's okay. If the trials are done right, we'll be out soon."

Scott smiled, "True. And then? You should be leading WorldStage, then."

She smiled again, "I would like to, in a democratic system. There should be a lawful election system in this nation, with the public choosing their representatives. I'd like to present myself as a potential choice for the people then. And if they think of me as the right person, I'll be doing my best to keep my promises to them, to honour their faith in me."

The helicopters were landing on the building rooftop. "Ma'am", someone said from the top, "Would you please come here for a second?"

"Coming.", She replied and looked at Scott, "Come on Scott, let's go."

The two started to walk towards the building, along with the cat. "What now?" Scott asked, taking one long look at the outside before entering the building.

"Now", Stana said, "We change the world."

[The End]

About the Author

Tathagata Banerjee

Tathagata Banerjee is a trilingual poet, author, novelist, short story writer, and translator. Some of his books include Diary of the Buddha Poet, Postcard from Memory Lane, Neon Sanjhbatir Dystopia, and more. For Ukiyoto, the author had penned Hurts that Hate You. Banerjee has also been published internationally and has presented his literary paper on cross-border webinars, too. For his work, he has received the 21st Century BookLeaf Emily Dickinson Award. Banerjee has also translated the works of iconic Bengali poets like Jibanananda Das and Sunil Gangopadhyay into English.

www.ingramcontent.com/pod-product-compliance
Lightning Source LLC
LaVergne TN
LVHW041556070526
838199LV00046B/2005